MERRY CHRISTMAS,
ALEX CROSS

BOOKS BY JAMES PATTERSON

FEATURING ALEX CROSS

A complete list of books by James Patterson is at the end of the book. For previews and more information about the author, visit JamesPatterson.com or find him on Facebook or at your app store.

MERRY CHRISTMAS, ALEX CROSS

JAMES PATTERSON

LITTLE, BROWN AND COMPANY

NEW YORK   BOSTON   LONDON

Copyright © 2011 by James Patterson

Little, Brown and Company
Hachette Book Group
237 Park Avenue, New York, NY 10017
www.hachettebookgroup.com

Little, Brown and Company is a division of Hachette Book Group, Inc. The Little, Brown name and logo are trademarks of Hachette Book Group, Inc.

The publisher is not responsible for websites (or their content) that are not owned by the publisher.

The Hachette Speakers Bureau provides a wide range of authors for speaking events. To find out more, go to www.hachettespeakersbureau.com or call (866) 376-6591.

ISBN 978-0-316-21073-7

10 9 8 7 6 5 4 3 2 1

Printed in the United States of America

Prologue
THE DEVIL ON CHRISTMAS EVE

ONE

A SMALL REAR DOOR TO ST. ANTHONY'S CHURCH HAD BEEN LEFT OPEN.
Exactly as I had been promised. My partner in crime,
John Sampson, and I walked in through the dark sacristy—the spacious room where they kept the altar
wine, hymnals, and vestments, and where the priests
dressed for services.

"Sugar, I hope we don't have to shoot somebody in
a church," Sampson said in a stage whisper.

"Especially on Christmas Eve in a church."

"Not funny, Alex."

"Who's laughing? Not me. Not in church."

We made our way along a short, narrow hallway that
led to the altar itself. Except for some flickering votive
candles, a few dim overheads, and a hanging candle
near the altar table itself, there was no other light in the
church.

It was early on Christmas Eve, and in the near
darkness the huge wreaths and balsam roping that
decorated the church looked a long way from festive.
If anything, St. Anthony's seemed depressing. And I

figured things were about to get worse, Christmas Eve or not.

I walked to the right side of the altar and stooped down low behind the carved oak pulpit. John went to the left side and knelt among the bright-red poinsettia plants. He had worn a red ski cap in preparation for…whatever was going to happen next.

Funny how a neighborhood church can feel so calm and safe, though, a true refuge. The statues, the flickering votive candles. It tells you that although there's a crazy world out there, inside all is calm and good.

But not today. Not for the two of us.

The late daylight sweeping through the stained glass made the statues seem crazy around the eyes, almost evil. The blood on the altar crucifix looked like human blood. An omen of things to come? I hoped not.

A whisper punctuated the darkness. Sampson among the poinsettias: "Is this what they mean when they say they're using a cop as a *plant?*"

I just shook my head, said not a word. Nothing like a bad pun to make the season full of both merry and ridiculous.

The church was silent again. The musty smell of old incense was everywhere. We waited for the action to start.

I thought back several decades ago, to the time I made my confirmation. That day the bishop standing before all of us twelve-year-old kids said, "Fill them with your spirit of fear, O Lord." And now I finally knew what he meant.

I was beside the altar with a gun on my hip. I was on a stakeout in my own family's church. I was filled with that spirit of fear, and keeping my eye on every shadowy corner, waiting for a real live devil to appear.

I stared out at the sparse congregation. No devils anywhere in sight. There couldn't have been more than three or four people in the place. An old woman saying her beads, a homeless guy catching a nap, an older man reading a prayer book and muttering curses. I carefully checked out each of them.

Then a young girl in a fur coat, a coat way too fancy for St. Anthony's, barged out of one of the confessional box's doors. She was sobbing into a long, striped crimson-and-gray scarf. The priest came out after her. Father Harris placed his hand on her shoulder and led her to a pew. The padre is a very nice guy, a good priest.

I kept studying the church, waiting for the devil to appear. A few more minutes of quiet passed. The older lady dropped her rosary beads. They echoed like a rock slide.

Silence. And more silence.

Then I saw someone come out from the *other* door of the confessional booth. This had to be our man.

He was a young guy, and he was a big guy. He slouched slowly up the center aisle as if he were deep in prayer, moving toward the main doors.

I signaled Sampson, and the two of us began walking up either side aisle. We appeared deep in thought too. But it wasn't prayer. We had our hands on our holstered guns.

The guy in question stopped at the holy water font in the rear. He dipped his left hand into the water and blessed himself. A left hand in holy water is a big no-no. *Right hand only.*

Sampson and I kept slowly, quietly making our way up the aisles. We were almost at the rear of the church now.

Then I saw what I had half expected: with his left hand blessing himself, he was using his right, and a screwdriver, to pry the top off a plain wooden container. The container was marked FOR THE POOR.

My voice shattered the church silence. "Let's get this sonofabitch!"

We had met the devil.

In church.

On Christmas Eve.

TWO

FATHER HARRIS FLIPPED ON THE POWER FLOODLIGHT, AND THE ENTIRE REAR of the church was suddenly bathed in white light. The devil was on the run. So were Sampson and I. We were on top of the perp the second he tried pushing open one of the carved doors to the outside.

I brought my clasped hands down like a hammer on his back. He grunted and dropped to the floor. I was on him. Then I pushed my knee hard into his stomach.

I let up, and Sampson rolled and cuffed him. What a team—ever since we were kids growing up together in Southeast.

I looked at my partner and said, "John, say Merry Christmas to our old friend Latrell Lewis."

"It *is* Lewis! Holy shit!" said Sampson, who remembered he was in a church and added, "Sorry about that, Jesus."

Latrell Lewis and I had had some unpleasant history together. It'd started five years ago when he was a fifteen-year-old bag messenger for one of the second-tier Columbia Heights gangs. His street name was Lit-Lat for "Little Latrell." The punk was arrogant enough to try going out on his own, and then stupid enough to get picked up by Sampson and me the first week he was flying solo. Next time we took him in, Latrell ended up in a lovely spot in Maryland, Jessup Correctional, for a year and a half in the country.

"I just assumed you were still resting up in Maryland," I said to him.

"Maybe you should learn to count—or buy yourself a calendar, Cross."

Sampson spoke. "You're lucky you're in a church. You see, I'm praying for patience, the patience not to shoot a warning shot into your leg. *Both* legs."

Then I added, "And remember, not all prayers are answered."

We pulled Lewis up off the floor. He was jittery, not just from nerves but from cocaine or heroin or whatever drug cocktail he was buying with church money. I really didn't care. I'm a psychologist, but I was in no mood to make a pro bono diagnosis and give the man some counseling.

"Come on. It's Christmas Eve. Show a brother a little heart," Lewis said.

"Yeah, we will," I answered. "We'll show you as much heart as you showed the folks who count on that poor-box money for food and shelter."

Then we hustled him through the big wooden church doors and out into the snow and the cold winter winds.

"C'mon, man. Don't put me in no police car. That'd be sad stuff for Christmas Eve."

I looked up at the white sky. Then I looked down at this punk junkie and said, "I don't want you to be sad, Latrell. So I'll tell you what. On the way down to the station house we can all sing Christmas carols."

Book One

MERRY CHRISTMAS, ALEX

CHAPTER

1

THEY SAY IT'S GOOD LUCK WHEN IT SNOWS ON CHRISTMAS EVE. I DON'T usually buy into that kind of folk wisdom, but if it turned out to be true, well, this would be one of the best Christmases ever. It was definitely looking to be some kind of record-breaking white Christmas. The snow was falling in big thick flakes. If you turned the city upside down, Washington would look just like one of those snow globes the tourists buy at Union Station and the airports.

Sampson and I brought Lewis in and booked him, and it looked like he'd be waiting for Santa in a holding cell this yuletide season. By the time I got home, it was close to eleven o'clock.

Bree and the kids were busy finishing trimming the tree. Official Sergeant of All Holidays Nana Mama was supervising every little task on her to-do list.

"Don't put two green ornaments right next to each other, Damon. Show some style when you decorate a tree," said my ninetysomething-year-old grandmother.

Bree was hooking a faded crayon drawing of the

three wise men on one of the branches. According to legend, I had made that ornament when I was in kindergarten, and Nana always dragged it out at Christmas.

"Well, look who's come in from the snowstorm," Bree said, and she walked over and gave me a sweet kiss on the lips. "Hello, sweetheart."

Nana decided not to look in my direction. All she said was "Is there a faint possibility, Alex, that you might spend a few minutes of the holiday season with your family? Or are we asking too much?"

I was dispensing hugs to Ali, Jannie, and Damon—home on winter break from prep school—and now Ava, the foster child Nana had recently brought under our roof. I should have had the wisdom to say nothing to Nana, just give her a Christmas kiss, but I'll never learn. She pushes my buttons like nobody else on this earth.

"Nana, this morning when I got a jingle from the pastor at St. Anthony's, Father Harris told me that *you* were the one who suggested he call me to help catch the poor-box thief," I said, *"which I did."*

"He said that?" Nana asked, not even cracking a smile at my accusation.

"He sure did. He said that he hated to pester me on Christmas Eve, but you had told him it would be no bother. Wouldn't take any time at all to solve the case of the poor-box pilferer."

"Imagine. A priest saying that. Father Harris of all people." She shook her head and said, "Here you go,

Ali. Put this porcelain Baby Jesus on a low branch. So if it falls it doesn't fall far."

"Are you telling a little fib on Christmas Eve, Nana?" I asked.

"I'm not telling anything to anyone. I'm just saying this: It would be pitiful that a man couldn't be with his family on Christmas Eve. Even a high-and-mighty homicide detective like yourself."

Everyone was chuckling at Nana's giving me such a hard time. I was holding back a smile myself. So was she.

Then Bree said, "I'll be right back," and she left the room. I had to admit that the tree looked pretty great against the snowy picture window. Then Bree reappeared with a big glass bowl of homemade eggnog, another Christmas Eve tradition in our house.

The eggnog had large globs of real whipped cream in it, so rich and sweet, each cupful must have registered a couple thousand calories. But, hey, it was the Christmas season. And even though Nana wouldn't stop riding me about working on Christmas Eve, it was setting up to be a warm, wonderful night at home.

Warm and wonderful for about ten minutes anyway.

Then my cell phone rang, and the sound seemed to suck the air out of the room. I answered and listened to the assistant chief of detectives. Then I announced to my family that I was really sorry. "I have to go in to work. I wasn't given a choice. It's a bad one."

Nana rolled her eyes. The kids looked away from me.

Bree just shook her head and said, "Merry Christmas, Alex. It's a bad one."

CHAPTER
2

DAMN IT TO HELL, I THOUGHT, AND I WAS SORRY TO BE THINKING LIKE THAT so close to Christmas. There's only one person in the world who should be working on Christmas. And he wears a goofy red suit and drinks way too much fattening eggnog topped with real whipped cream. *Damn it, and damn Santa too.*

As I drove through the almost deserted DC streets, the snow that had looked so beautiful an hour ago seemed absolutely ugly and annoying. It was depressing to leave my house and family, and I didn't blame them for being angry and upset with me. Hell, I was angry and upset with me. And with my job.

After a few skids and spins—I guess the city DPW snowplow folks were home with *their* families—I was in Georgetown. I made a left turn and started to look for the address on 30th Street NW.

I had no trouble finding it. A beautiful limestone house was lit up like the White House Christmas tree. But most of the lighting effects were coming from police cars, flashlights, floodlights, and network TV camera lights. *Oh yeah, Merry Christmas, Alex.*

I had left home so quickly that I didn't even think to pull on a pair of snow boots. My shoes began filling up with chunks of ice and wet snow as I slogged toward the crime scene.

Out of nowhere a middle-aged man in a green ski parka and red ski hat walked up to me. The guy pulled off his gloves and held out a puffy red hand.

"You're Alex Cross, aren't you?" he said.

"I'm him. And you're…?" I thought I knew most cops in DC, but this one—with the sea of freckles and bits of wavy red hair sneaking out from his ski hat—was new to me.

"Detective Tom McGoey. Six whole days with the MPD. Originally from Staten Island."

"Happy holidays, Detective. Welcome to Washington. Now can you tell me what's going on here?"

"I'll do my best—but I'm afraid I have one helluva awful Christmas gift for you."

I nodded. "Yeah, I already figured that much. Let's hear it."

3

McGOEY BEGAN TO EXPLAIN WHAT WAS GOING ON, AND IT CLEARLY WAS A god-awful situation, one that could turn into a full-scale tragedy.

The beautiful Georgetown house that we were standing in front of had once belonged to Henry Fowler. Now it belonged to Fowler's former wife, Diana. She was living there with their eleven-year-old twins, Jeremy and Chloe, and their six-year-old son, Trey. Oh yeah—and her new husband.

"They're all hostages inside the house. Fowler's also got Melissa Brandywine in there. She's the next-door neighbor," McGoey said.

"Is she related to Congressman Brandywine, the mogul from Northern California?" I asked.

McGoey nodded. "Yeah, she's the congressman's wife. She was supposed to be flying to Aspen tomorrow morning to join the husband and their three kids skiing. But she had the bad luck to drop off homemade cookies today for her neighbors."

Funny how a nice small-town gesture can turn rotten in DC.

Then McGoey gave me some intel that shed more light on how we all got to be standing outside the house in a snowstorm on Christmas.

It seems that Mrs. Fowler had remarried in the fall. She was now Mrs. Nickleson, wife of Dr. Barry Nickleson, a teaching ophthalmologist at George Washington.

And Henry Fowler, her ex, was now one crazy pissed-off dude.

"That's what we know so far. The background check on Fowler should be here in a few. As you might have guessed, headquarters isn't exactly loaded with personnel tonight," McGoey said.

"What's Fowler got aimed at the hostages?" I asked.

"Enough shit to invade China."

Colorful answer, I thought. But I was hoping for something a little more specific. I assumed that Fowler was crazy, but I wanted to figure out if he was crazy-crazy or smart-crazy. McGoey elaborated on his one-liner.

"He's got a Glock Nineteen," he said. "With a second Glock for backup."

That's the standard-issue gun of the MPD. The good thing about a 19 is that it holds seventeen rounds. The bad thing about a 19 is that it holds seventeen rounds.

"Then he's got two Walther G-Twenty-two semi-automatic rifles."

Another street weapon.

"Fowler's also got around two hundred spare mags for the G-Twenty-twos."

I asked the obvious question. "How'd you find out what Fowler has for fire?"

"He was good enough to tell us during our first and only intervention phone call," McGoey said.

"So that's the whole arsenal?" I asked. "I hope?"

"No, it isn't. We're just warming up."

Why did I think that McGoey was getting some special pleasure in watching me get shakier as he spoke? Maybe because that's the way *he* was feeling?

"He's got two AR-Fifteen carbine rifles."

Two of everything. Was that part of a plan, or was Fowler just obsessive-compulsive about doing things in pairs?

"He's got two M-Sixty-one hand grenades, two semis—and two peanut-butter-and-jelly sandwiches."

I didn't know what McGoey's sense of humor was like, but I didn't think the sandwich joke was all that funny.

"Listen—," I started, but McGoey interrupted me.

"Let me explain. The twins are fatally allergic to peanuts. One bite of a pbj sandwich, and in five minutes they won't be breathing."

CHAPTER
4

THERE'S SOMETHING I LEARNED A LONG TIME AGO WORKING HOMICIDE: AN in-family hostage situation is hands-down, absolutely, no-argument, the worst kind of situation. You might be able to sharpshoot a terrorist. Or meticulously unravel a kidnapping. I have outfoxed a serial killer or two. But someone holding family members hostage is a great big Mack truck of insanity. The guy doesn't give a damn about his hostages or his future. It's a lose-lose situation.

And as for police negotiators, well, they're trained and they're usually smart, but life isn't anything like television. Have I ever seen a hostage-taker listen to a negotiator and then throw down his weapon and come out with his hands up? Sure, as often as I've seen Santa Claus and his reindeer land on somebody's roof. Could happen. Not likely.

I followed Detective McGoey over to a police van. It was parked on the front lawn of a brick Georgian Colonial across the street from the hostage scene.

"Whose property did we take over?" I asked McGoey.

"Ambassador from Nigeria. I have no idea how to pronounce the name."

"Nice place he's got," I said. "The ambassador's name is Uwem Naikye."

"Yeah, half his country is starving to death, and this dude's living in six bedrooms in Georgetown. Guess he's gone for the holidays too."

"Yeah, in Lagos. I've been there, but not for the holidays. From the look of things, maybe I'd rather be in Lagos tonight myself."

CHAPTER

5

A MAJOR-LEAGUE EMERGENCY SETUP WAS HIDDEN BEHIND THE MPD VAN.
Two speakers let everyone hear what was being said on
the phone line between the van and the house, which
had a low-tech speakerphone.

The only problem was that Fowler wouldn't answer
the phone. Not lately anyway.

So a half dozen cops were standing around pressing
phone buttons like lunatics, waiting for a madman to
pick up. A few lucky dogs like McGoey and me got to
stand behind the police van under a thick tarp that had
been set up to offer some protection from the snow and
howling wind.

Lieutenant Adam Nu was part of the scene, and that
was a good thing. Nu was cautious and very smart. He
was also a good friend of mine. We played racquetball
together. Adam had set up a good solid fort here. Ten of
his men were angled at different distances and locations
around the Fowler house. Others had taken up window positions in surrounding homes. The snow made
it impossible to put our people on the roofs—the ideal

location. It also blocked the snipers' views of the target. Several body-armored SWAT members were ready to rush in if hell broke loose, which was definitely a possibility. More so as the night wore on.

I watched two SWAT officers constantly circling the house. They each carried a SIG SAUER P226 sidearm, and a Stoner SR-25 high-powered sniper rifle. No self-respecting hostage-taker would want to be the target of an SR-25.

"Shouldn't those officers with the SIGs be standing still—like everyone else?" McGoey asked.

"No. We used to do it that way," I said. "But research from the FBI showed that moving shooters keep the perp off guard. Sometimes confuses him."

Before I could say anything more, Diego Ramiro, the hostage negotiator, shouted, "Goddamn it, I give up. I can't do anything, nothing, if this sonofabitch won't talk to me on the phone!"

I'd worked with Ramiro before. He wasn't one to lose his cool. Maybe it was happening because it was Christmas and he was working a hotline.

I said, "How long have we been calling Fowler?"

Diego flipped through his notepad. "Since nine thirty, Alex. Almost four hours ago."

McGoey said, "That's when Fowler was real chatty about who he had in there and all his guns and ammo. The guy hasn't picked up the phone since. Not the house phone. Not his cell. Not anyone else's cell."

Diego Ramiro kept dialing. Four other police officers kept dialing. Each time, they either were cut off or got voice mail.

The messages the police left came out over the speakers like a crazy word symphony, something like: "Please… Mr…. Please… Mr…. Fowler…. This can… be… Mr. Fowler… children…. It's your chance… hurt… harm…. They love you… need help… you need help…. "

I pulled out my cell and then looked at the list of phone numbers taped to the side of the van. I dialed the home number of the house under siege. Then I had a thought: *This is just like when Bree's car won't start on an icy morning. I'll go out to her and say, "Let me try," and Bree'll say, "What makes you think that you turning the ignition key is going to work any better than me turning the ignition key?" And, of course, she's right.*

And, of course, my phone call went unanswered just like the hundreds of calls that had preceded it.

But the moment I hung up, Diego shouted, "I think someone finally picked up in there!"

Sure enough, voices suddenly came from the speakers. They were muffled, indistinguishable at first. We held our collective breaths and stared at the speakers as if they were video monitors.

I tried hard to figure out what was being said. No luck. Then I heard something that was easy to understand.

Six gunshots—in stereo—coming from the house and from the speakers. The Christmas horror show had begun…or maybe it had just ended.

CHAPTER
6

DAMON WAS STANDING ON TIPTOE ON A WOBBLY KITCHEN CHAIR. HE WAS sweating and trying very hard to hook a delicate antique angel to the top of the Christmas tree.

Damon repeated that he didn't need a stepladder to get the angel up there. Nana Mama said he *did* need a stepladder but he was just too lazy to go to the broom closet and get it.

Finally the lovely white-and-powder-blue angel was secured.

"A little applause, if you don't mind," Damon said. "For the angel, and for me."

But nobody felt much like applauding or laughing. Nobody was feeling very good about Christmas since Alex left the house.

As Bree and the children packed away the decorations they wouldn't be using—broken ornaments and strings of lights that didn't light—Nana said, "You know, I don't understand why the top of the tree is always the last thing we decorate. It should be the first thing we do. So the angel can look down on us while we decorate the tree. That makes perfect sense, doesn't it?"

Nobody joined the conversation, but Nana kept going. "Jannie, what do you think?" she asked.

"With all due respect, Nana, I think that you think that if you keep talking we'll forget that Dad is out on a case. And that he might get hurt on Christmas."

Nana walked to Jannie and hugged her tightly. "You are one smart girl, Jannie. Smart women run in this family."

Bree smiled slightly, and Nana tried her hardest to snap back into her sensible self. She said, "That Alex. It's all my fault. I didn't raise him right. If I did he'd never be foolish enough to go out on a nasty case on Christmas."

Again, nobody said a word. They all realized that Nana was doing everything in her considerable power to get everyone to feel good again. But it wouldn't work this time. They understood that Alex—a good husband, a father, a grandson—was out in the snowstorm doing his job, and the only thing they could do was worry until he returned safe and sound.

Then Bree spoke.

"Listen, it's pretty obvious that Alex won't be home for a while. Maybe quite a while. So let's all get to bed and get some rest. Merry Christmas to all."

Ava added, "And to all a good night." And Bree smiled. Then she saw that Nana's eyes were filling with tears.

"Yes," Nana said. "A good night. Please, Dear Lord, let it be a good night."

CHAPTER

7

SIX HOSTAGES. AND NOW SIX RAPID-FIRE GUNSHOTS.

"I took out every one of them! Every one of those sad pieces of shit!" A male voice came over the speaker—loud, and angry, and ugly, like the voice of a devil.

Just in case we couldn't figure it out for ourselves, McGoey said, "That's Henry Fowler screaming."

Coming loud and clear through the speakers, along with Fowler's crazy voice, were the piercing cries of children and the frightened voices of adults. At least they were alive. Some of them anyway.

Now Fowler was laughing—the laugh of the happy madman.

"There! There's a Merry Christmas for you. The hostages are still alive!"

A different male voice could be heard. *Dr. Nickleson?* "How? Why?...All these toys. Gifts..."

Another blast. Then Fowler: "Shut the hell up, Doc, or you'll be lying next to the busted gifts. I *want* to shoot *you!*"

I was getting a hint of what had just happened. Then Henry Fowler confirmed it.

"Don't anybody worry out there. All is well, all is good, all is holy. These scumbuckets are still alive in here. But the shit that Santa left under the tree is totally deceased. Rest in peace, useless, expensive crap."

McGoey shook his head in disbelief. But I didn't. Nothing was too crazy to imagine in a hostage situation like this one.

"So what did Henry F. and his magical gun take out?" Fowler said with squeaky "pity" in his voice.

"*Awww.* A nice new iPad. Got it right in the apple…and here we have what used to be an Xbox 360. You should be thanking me, Jeremy. Now you'll have more time for your homework.…Sorry to ruin whatever was in that little Tiffany box, sweetheart.…And that beautiful blue Polo sweater. It's just too bad you weren't wearing it, Doc.…"

The laugh that Fowler let out was part scream and part cackle. *Another gunshot!* Then Fowler said, "That stupid ornament with the twins' baby picture. I always hated that ornament."

I held up my hand to the people surrounding the outside speakers. I pointed to myself and made a gesture to indicate that I was going to talk to him.

"Hey, Mr. Fowler," I said calmly, carefully, almost softly—the way I'd been taught.

"Who the hell are *you?*" Fowler shot back.

I remembered not to use the word *detective.* "This is

Alex Cross. I'm glad to hear that the people you've got in there are okay. That's good news."

Fowler exploded. "What are you, *another dumb-ass cop?* These people in here are *not* doing okay. They're about to get their goddamn heads blown off."

I persisted. Calmly. *Calmly.*

"I understand what you're saying. How about I put Mr. Ramiro back on? You and he might be able to work some things out."

Calmly. Calmly.

"You talking about that cop negotiator?" Fowler asked.

"Yes," I said.

"Let me tell you this: I am absolutely not talking to that whiny little asshole again. *Ever.*"

Click.

CHAPTER

8

THIS WAS GETTING WORSE AS THE SNOWFALL THICKENED. ADAM NU SEEMED to be on the phone every few minutes with Congressman Brandywine. A snowstorm out West had stranded him in Aspen. And here at the other end of the world, the DC weather wasn't exactly conducive to easy jet landings.

So when I saw Adam walking quickly toward us from one of the police cars, I assumed it had something to do with Brandywine. It didn't.

"Detectives," Adam said as he joined us under the tarp, "I've got to show you something you won't like to see."

He abruptly snapped open his PowerBook and continued, "Downtown MPD just sent us the background information on Henry Fowler."

"The bottom line?" I asked.

"My initial analysis is pretty simple: Fowler's a fucking maniac on wheels! He's gone off the res, and he ain't coming back."

McGoey and I leaned over Nu's shoulder and began

reading the Christmas card that headquarters had just sent us. It confirmed Adam's opinion.

Fowler's life had started off overflowing with promise—New Trier High, supposedly a good public school in the Chicago suburbs, then Georgetown undergraduate, Georgetown Law. The MPD even managed to dig up Fowler's college yearbook photo. He had graduated third in his class, and it sure didn't hurt that he looked like he could be Tom Brady's brother.

Then Fowler landed at Jordan Haig, one of the best white-shoe law firms in town. He was a defense lawyer with that perfect combination of classic eloquence and the killer attitude to "do whatever it takes to win the case."

I actually remembered Fowler now. He'd handled a class-action suit that made a lot of headlines: nine hundred women were suing a drug chain for noncompetitive wages and workplace harassment. Bree followed the case almost obsessively. She believed the women had been horribly treated.

Fowler represented the drug chain, and Fowler won.

He seemed to specialize in drug-related cases. He had defended one of the big New Jersey companies against charges that their new hepatitis-A drug caused neurological damage in 10 percent of the users. Fowler won again. The drug stayed on the market.

"Now here's where it all starts to unravel—all because of one event," said Nu, pointing to a single line: *Fowler v. Fowler.* "That's from a few years ago, when Diana Fowler filed for divorce."

Nu was right. Henry Fowler's life had roared completely off the tracks. The obvious assumption was that he just couldn't handle his wife leaving him for another man. Whatever the cause, almost every week the MPD blotter had something interesting to report about Fowler.

Charges of spousal abuse. Charges of child abuse.

Illegal possession of firearms. DUI three times. Driver's license suspended.

Breaking and entering in Georgetown. Fowler arrested and released. "He must have been a buddy of the judge," Nu said. "No way he should've gotten out of that one."

Then assault with a deadly weapon. Fowler had stormed into Dr. Nickleson's office at GWU and held him captive for an hour and a half. Fowler was arrested. But Nickleson refused to bring charges. The police couldn't get "unlawful entry" or "kidnapping" to stick without Nickleson's agreement.

Things got even worse from there.

Around the time of the assault on his ex-wife's boyfriend, Fowler was told to take a leave of absence at Jordan Haig. A few days later he was picked up for possession of drugs—four grams of heroin. Lucky guy: he had his three-month sentence suspended. Not-so-lucky guy: he also had his license to practice law suspended.

Like they say on the late-night infomercials, "But wait. There's more." Hard to imagine, but Fowler tried to become a drug dealer. Instead, he became a small-time hustler. He lived on the street for a while, the usual elegant lodging—Dumpsters, abandoned houses, public restrooms. Then a third-rate hooker named Patty (MPD couldn't find a last name for her) took him in. This was no hot congressional call girl either. Patty was a pathetic druggie. The shakes, rotted teeth, HIV, the whole drug catalog of problems. She and Fowler spent most of their days shooting up.

Fowler, however, did make some time to hang around his kids' schools, his ex-wife's house, and the GWU campus, trying to scare the shit out of everyone he held responsible for his downfall. Of course, all involved got protection orders against him. The orders were for three months. The three months ended in mid-December.

"Jesus!" McGoey said. "There's a charmed life that zoomed straight into the toilet. He must have really loved that wife of his."

The psychologist in me thought differently. "Maybe he didn't love her. Maybe he just hated the new husband. Hated losing control of his wife. And the family."

McGoey and Nu nodded. No one spoke. No one spoke because they were waiting for me to say something else.

"So what do you think?" McGoey finally asked. "Can we get them out of there in one piece?"

"To be honest, I was thinking of something an old boss of mine used to say. There's no snooze button on a human time bomb."

CHAPTER
9

THE TEAM HUDDLED—TOM McGOEY, ADAM NU, THE PISSED-OFF NEGOTIATOR Diego Ramiro, the two SWAT team guys who had been circling the house, two more SWAT team guys who were sniper experts, and…oh yeah…me.

"You called the meeting, Alex," Nu said. "What are you thinking?"

"It's pretty simple, I guess. A rookie would probably come to the same conclusion. If we don't rush the house soon, Fowler shoots everybody. Or best case—he stays holed up in there until Easter, which is almost as bad."

McGoey looked to the SWAT team members. "You got anything that could help us?"

The first guy, a small tough-looking Asian, said, "Well, we couldn't place the Minicam anywhere useful. Too much freaking snow and ice. Plus Fowler is jumping around in there like a jackrabbit. He'd have seen us—and who knows who he would have ended up shooting."

"But speaking of ice, we can tell you this," said his

partner, a blond guy who looked more like a stoner than a member of a SWAT team, "Fowler is drugged up from here to hell. Maybe on super ice."

He was referring to crystal meth, and it was in the write-up we'd gotten on Fowler. In prison, meth was passed around like an hors d'oeuvre at a party. In the last few years it had become just as popular on the streets of DC.

"Smoke or needle?" Nu asked the group. "Makes a difference."

"Needle," the stoner dude answered without hesitation.

"Then I worry he might stick a dirty hypo in one of the hostages," McGoey said.

"Ice users don't like to share," the stoner said.

"Yeah, why waste perfectly good meth on someone when you can just shoot 'em?" agreed Nu.

According to the workup, and from the way the SWAT team guys described Fowler's behavior, he was a walking, talking example of what meth could do—violent behavior; paranoia; uncontrolled euphoria, then uncontrolled depression.

"Okay," I said. "Sounds like we've got to get in there. One way or the other."

"Agreed. I'd do it the tried-and-sometimes-true way," said Nu. "Alert the shooters up in the other houses. Put our people at as many ground-floor windows as we can cover. Position SWAT at every door—front, back, patio, kitchen, garage. Distract Fowler at the front door—that's where they reflexively fix their attention—and then we go in through the back."

Adam Nu paused. He was actually sweating. The snow was falling hard. The thermometer read about twenty-five, but beads of perspiration covered his forehead. I realized I was sweating too.

"Let's talk about timing," I said. "And let's discuss it right now. The longer we wait—"

Then I saw something that made me stop midsentence.

Over Nu's shoulder I noticed a woman tromping through the snow. She was walking right toward us. It was Bree. *What's wrong? Why is Bree here?*

CHAPTER
10

"EXCUSE ME, GENTLEMEN. I'LL BE RIGHT BACK," I SAID AS I BROKE AWAY from the group. Maybe it's my police mentality, but when someone shows up unexpectedly, I always assume it means bad news. And I'm often right.

"Bree, it's almost three in the morning. There's a snowstorm. What are you doing here?" I asked.

"Did you think I could possibly sleep, Alex? I called in to the precinct house to get the location," she said. "I came over...to see how it's going."

I hugged her tightly for a second. Then I held her by the shoulders and looked straight into her eyes.

"Now that you've seen the situation and have heard from me that it's bad, really bad, why don't you go back home?"

"Only if you'll go with me," she said with a half smile. "That's the deal I'm offering. It's a pretty good deal."

"You're married to a cop, Bree."

"So are you, Alex. So don't try to play me. That never works, sweetheart."

She was always too smart. She knew that I was trying to calm her down any way I could, and it wasn't going to work.

"It's Christmas. Is it right that your family should be lying in bed, worrying about whether you're going to show up alive or dead?"

"Of course it's not right. But I've got to do it. You know that. Like you said, you're a cop. This is the job."

Bree pressed her wet, chilly cheek against my own. I couldn't care less if people were watching us and talking. How I wanted to be safely tucked into bed next to her. I held her for another moment. Then I let go.

Softly she said, "Just remember. It's Christmas, and you've got a family who loves you. Do you have any idea how much we love you? How much we're hurting?"

I nodded. Then I motioned with a hand toward the houseful of hostages.

"There's a family in there too," I said. "Unfortunately. I have to try and get them out."

Bree's eyes were filled with a mixture of understanding and anger. She touched my cheek again. Then she moved away. I watched her walk toward her car. She turned back and mouthed the words *I love you. Be careful. Christmas.*

CHAPTER
11

FINALLY I TURNED AWAY AND HEADED BACK TO THE GROUP. I DID KNOW HOW much my family loved me—so what was I doing here? What was I doing?

McGoey was holding a phone and moving toward me. Nu was right behind him. Something was going on again.

"It's Fowler. He wants to talk to you," McGoey said.

"Me?"

"You're Alex Cross, right?" Nu said.

I took the phone.

"Henry Fowler?" I said.

"Is this that sonofabitch, Detective Alex Cross?" he asked. "I know who you are. I guess I should be honored you're here at our block party."

I knew how I had to handle this. I had to stay calm. So Fowler wouldn't go crazy. But I also knew that I'd get nowhere if I didn't go shot for shot with him.

"What's the deal, Fowler?" I said in a quiet voice.

"There's no deal, Cross. Not for a while anyway. I'm having fun right now."

I shut my eyes. That wasn't what I wanted to hear.

This was going to be a long Christmas night.

"I thought we could make some contact. But a word of advice before we go any further," he said quietly, reasonably. A pause—and then he was suddenly screaming over the phone. "Don't fuck with me, Cross! Don't lie to me. *And don't fuck with me. Got it?*"

I kept my voice steady. "I've got it, Fowler. But here's a word of advice for you. Before we go any further. You can talk. And I promise I'll listen. I'll really listen. But now…here's the important part…I'll listen…*up to a point.*"

"When do we get to that *point?*" he asked.

I was taking a chance with my answer.

"When I say so."

A silence, and then Fowler spoke again.

"Okay, Detective Cross. We've got the start of a deal."

Then he exploded again, but not at me.

"I swear, this whiny kid better shut the hell up, Diana. *Shut her up! Now!*"

Through the phone I could hear a child crying hysterically. It was obviously Chloe, one of the twins. I could also hear Diana Fowler Nickleson saying, "Henry, for God's sake, you animal, you terrible person. Chloe's scared. She's tired. Your daughter is hungry."

Without missing a beat, and with cold sarcasm in his voice, Fowler said, "If she's hungry tell her to eat the sandwich I brought." Then he gave a sickening snicker. "Peanut butter, her favorite."

Diana again. "Henry—"

"Shut the hell up, *Diana!*" Fowler screamed. "I have no reason, and frankly no desire, to talk to you!"

Then two gunshots.

In his calm voice, Fowler said, "There goes your precious Japanese vase and your *cute* little crystal cigarette box, Diana. I just want you to fully understand: this entire gaudy room is nothing but a great big shooting gallery to me."

Then Nickleson's voice: "What's wrong with you, Fowler? You're nothing but—"

Another gunshot. Children crying, no other sounds.

Then Fowler returned to his crazy screaming voice. "Listen, you pathetic quack! You're the one I *most* want to put in the grave. Do you understand that? You're the one I want to kill. Do you understand that?"

No answer from Dr. Nickleson.

Then Fowler screamed, *"Do you fucking understand that?"*

"Listen to him, Barry. Please listen," said Diana.

"I'm listening," said the doctor softly. "And of course I understand."

Now Fowler spoke with quiet and controlled rage. "Let me make this clear. No one in this room should have anything to say, not anything. Not a word. But that's especially true of you, quackster. So listen to me carefully. Very carefully. If you say one more word, just one… more…word…even a cough…even a hiccup…I'm going to kill you. Nod your head if you understand the rules."

I assumed that Dr. Nickleson nodded.

Then, as if he were returning to a business call at the office, Fowler said, "Hey, Cross. Sorry to keep you holding on like that."

I jumped in now with a very big request. A game changer, maybe.

"Hey, listen, Fowler. I was wondering if I could come in the house and join you," I said matter-of-factly. I was going for a kind of "could I borrow your lawn mower" style. Never up, never in.

There was a long pause. Then, to my surprise, I heard Fowler say, "Why would you want to do that, Cross?"

"Well, I want to hear what you have to say about this situation. And I think it might be done better in person."

Another pause. That pause stretched into thirty seconds. The thirty seconds stretched into the longest minute of my life.

My fear was that Fowler was about to explode with rage again, and then he could turn his guns on the hostages. I could see McGoey shaking his head as if he *knew* I was making the wrong move.

Finally Fowler did speak.

"I don't think so, Cross. Nice try, but I don't think so."

Persistence. Persistence.

"It would give me the opportunity to hear your side of the story. I have an idea that there's some justification for your anger."

Another few seconds.

Then Fowler said very quietly, very calmly, "One simple rule: if I frisk you when you come in, and I find you're carrying a gun, I'm going to kill you. And I'll kill a hostage or two. Starting with the good doctor."

"I don't need a gun to have a conversation," I said, and I handed my Glock to McGoey.

Fifteen seconds passed. Then Fowler's voice came again.

"Jeremy, go open the front door. I'm going to be right behind you, buddy. So don't even think about running out of the house. Understand?

"Okay, get going." But I guess the boy didn't go fast enough, because then I heard this father, on Christmas Eve, shout at his eleven-year-old son, "Move your fat ass, Jeremy, or *I'll fucking kill you.*"

I looked at my watch. It was almost four a.m.

I began walking toward the house.

CHAPTER

12

WHILE I'D BEEN ON THE PHONE WITH FOWLER, NU AND McGOEY HAD BEEN putting the "storm and protect" operation into place. As I crossed 30th Street I saw that the SWAT officers had started circling the house again. Only this time their weapons were cocked and carried in the underarm position. They were ready for trouble, for anything that might happen in the next few minutes. Like me getting shot.

The second and third floors of the surrounding houses were manned with sharpshooters. Inside those four houses, lights flicked on and off slowly.

Signals were being exchanged, but I couldn't begin to understand what they meant. I had other problems to figure out, and figure out fast.

In a few seconds I was directly facing the house. My eyes darted to the right and saw police officers quickly moving the news reporters back and away. They didn't have to ask twice, which told me that everybody saw this for the extremely dangerous situation it was.

I began walking up the short entrance path. The

big front door, framed with small frosted glass windows, was barely cracked open. The ankle-high snow, of course, had not been cleared. My shoes and feet were soaked through with water and ice. My toes and heels already hurt from the cold.

From inside the house I heard kids crying, a woman weeping. Suddenly lights were turned off—front rooms, hallway, outdoor lights. Total blackout.

As I took one step up onto the brick entrance platform, the front door seemed to open as if by magic. A dark entry hall loomed straight ahead. Then I saw the figure of a child running through the darkness and disappearing toward the left.

The night was so quiet that for one crazy moment I thought I could hear the snowflakes landing on the ground. I stepped into the front hallway and immediately heard Fowler's angry-crazy voice. He sounded nervous now. He was breathing heavily. Not good signs. The house lights went on again.

"Merry Christmas, Cross."

"Same to you," I said.

"Hope I didn't make a mistake letting you into the house."

"Well, that makes two of us," I said.

He told me to close the door and lock it.

And once again I wondered, *What am I doing here?*

CHAPTER

13

IT LOOKED LIKE SOMEONE HAD FOUGHT A SMALL WAR IN THE LIVING ROOM on 30th Street NW, Washington, DC. It also looked like the winner had taken six hostages alive. Three children and three adults lay on their bellies on the floor. They watched me from ground level.

I could feel the pleading hope and fear in their eyes, eyes that were red from fatigue and tension and crying. Diana Nickleson was wearing nothing but jeans and a bra. I had no idea what that was all about. Her new husband, who looked like a dark-haired version of her old husband, wore a pair of red corduroy pants. His green sweater had been slit down the back. I had no idea what that was about either.

Lots of mysteries to be solved.

Melissa Brandywine was lying between Nickleson and his wife. Melissa was a society-page regular. She had long copper-colored hair that could have used some time in the salon right about now. She was shaking uncontrollably. I couldn't blame her. Her life was in danger. *Why has Fowler involved her?*

The kids were an even sorrier sight than the grown-ups, maybe because they were kids. Maybe because it was Christmas. Maybe because this sort of thing shouldn't be happening to anyone, anytime, at any age.

Henry Fowler stared at me for an uncomfortable few seconds. His face was a cold sneer. I liked him even less now that I'd met him.

"You have time for a joke?" he asked. "Lighten things up a bit? Holiday spirit and all that."

He really *was* crazy.

"This man," he began, "is sitting on the veranda with his wife. Beautiful sunset. He's sipping a delicious glass of burgundy. He says, 'I love you.' The wife looks over, and she says, 'Is that you talking, or is it the wine?' He looks at her. 'Actually, I was talking to the wine.' "

Fowler gazed around the room. Nobody was laughing. If anything, they were even more terrified than before he began his joke.

"Okay, well, have you met my Christmas guests, Cross? Let me introduce you," Fowler said next.

"Stop it!" Diana screamed. "You've got to stop this, Henry. At least let the children go."

"Don't be a poop, Diana. Show the spirit of the season." Fowler waved her off.

I couldn't let this go any further. "This is your family, Fowler. Your kids are right here. Look at them."

He turned on me and leveled the pistol. "Watch your mouth, Cross…and, oh yes, *that reminds me.* Legs apart, hands up against the wall."

I did as I was told.

When I placed my hands against the wall, I was looking into a photograph of two people on a rocky beach. Diana and Barry laughing and hugging on a perfect sunny day.

When Fowler finished frisking me, he said, "Glad to see you kept your word."

"I'd have been a fool not to."

"And there's no fool like a dead fool."

As I turned around I took in the rest of the ravaged room. A large Christmas tree was on its side, branches crushed, ornaments shattered, lights out. The debris from the earlier shoot-up of the gifts was everywhere, the remnants almost unrecognizable: pieces of aluminum from the iPad, bits of gold from whatever Nickleson had wrapped in the Tiffany box. Alongside a few of the fallen broken ornaments were two grenades. They looked like ornaments created by a lunatic.

Two rifles rested against the fireplace. Right under the stockings hung from the chimney with care.

I heard a child's voice behind me. It was Jeremy. "Mister, can you ask Daddy to go back to his house?"

Before I could deliver any words of comfort, Fowler walked and jammed his black-booted foot on the boy's ear.

"Shut up, Jeremy. I told you. I'm going no place, no place but here. You're my family!"

Then Fowler looked at me, smiled, and said, "Kids. They never listen."

If I peered hard enough into Henry Fowler's face, I could see the handsome young man from his college photographs. But a lot of life had happened between college and this Christmas night. Fowler's teeth looked rotted, and a few were missing. His blond hair grew in random chunky tufts. He was thin to the point of boniness, malnourishment—what Nana called *alcohol skinny*.

Henry Fowler was also a catalog of tics and twitches—squeezing his nose, scratching his head, massaging the back of his neck, biting the side of his index finger. If he sat next to you on the subway, you'd stand up quickly and move away, maybe to another car.

"So, I do want to talk to you, Cross. I truly do, but you know, it is imperative that you meet the people who so rudely say they don't want to meet you. So let's begin. May I call you Alex? Or do you prefer the honorific *Detective?* Or maybe Earl or Count or sir or Prince…"

His words were coming faster now, coming with the easy smoothness of a topflight defense attorney. The phrases jumped and stormed around; this madman had some polish and brains, which made him even scarier to me.

"Everybody stand up!" Fowler shouted at the six people on the floor. "Hurry up. Stand up." For extra emphasis he gave Dr. Nickleson a kick to the shoulder. They all struggled to their feet.

"Let's start the introductions."

CHAPTER

14

FOWLER'S VOICE WAS THICK WITH SARCASM AS HE SAID, "I WOULD LIKE to begin with the most important person in my life, my wife, Diana. Aha, you say, she's no longer my wife. Well, to that I say she vowed publicly to be my wife…until death do us part. As we attorneys say, *in perpetuity*.

"You ask, who is this woman named Diana? Let me tell you.

"Diana is that woman at the Sotheby's jade auction, bidding far too much for a ten-thousand-dollar green statue of a water buffalo, or yak, I'm not sure which. Diana is that woman who sets her authentic Regency dining table with two-thousand-dollar James Robinson place settings. Diana is that woman they fawn over at Bloomies and Bergdorf Goodman, the woman whose skinny little ass they kiss at Prada, the woman they serve tea to in private rooms at Tiffany's in Washington *and* New York. Yes, she's quite the gal.

"Diana is that woman who was buying nineteenth-century fine art while she was fucking that eyeglass maker over there. Diana is that woman who pissed away so very much of our money and then pissed away our marriage. All so she could fuck the guy who makes a living saying, *Now, can you read the next line? Now, what about the line under that?* This inconsequential little shit and my wife even had a standing reservation for a room at the Four Seasons Hotel. They screwed out what few brains they had at a fancy-ass hotel. And I paid the tab! You know what else, Cross? If you stand on the roof of my house, you can see the very place where they did their dirty business. The hotel where this nobody stole from me my wife…and my life…and my whole reason for living!"

Fowler was screaming now, his face bright red. He paced the room and grabbed at his head and neck. He nervously scratched his arms and chest. Nickleson remained steely-eyed. Melissa Brandywine looked like she was in a trance and about ready to fall asleep. The children? I felt that they might lose it at any moment. And Diana? She was completely expressionless.

"Are you beginning to understand what's going on here, Mr. Cross, Prince Cross, King Cross? Do you see who the victim is now?"

I said nothing. I just looked at Fowler and tried to seem objective. There would be no stopping his rant. He pointed to Melissa Brandywine.

"Now, you may be wondering who this lucky holiday guest is. Well, show Mr. Cross your pretty face, Missy. I said, *Show him your face.*"

He grabbed her by the chin, squeezing her hard.

"Show him the big phony smile that helped get your husband elected to Congress. While you're at it, show him the money! Show him your net worth statement. Show him your father's money, the money that actually got your husband elected to Congress." Now he was screaming again. "I said, *Show him your face!*"

Melissa Brandywine lifted her smeared, sad face and turned her head toward me. She looked so sad and broken and embarrassed. I had to wonder why.

"Yeah, that's the face. The face that's at all those White House luncheons, the face that's at all those embassy receptions. Oh, and one other thing. You probably didn't know this, Detective. Not too many people do actually. That face has been in bed next to me. It's been in bed next to me about, oh, twenty times. Don't tell Representative Brandywine that his wife was sleeping with the next-door neighbor. No, better not tell Congressman Brandywine. And, by all means, better not tell Congressman Brandywine's boyfriend." He spat out the word *boyfriend* with joy.

Suddenly Diana yelled out, "The children! Henry! *Our children!*"

And to my astonishment…Fowler stopped ranting.

Everything was suddenly quiet in the room, eerily quiet.

The six hostages stood at attention, almost frozen in place. Even the kids.

I thought I could hear the snowflakes again.

Fowler walked quickly to a sofa that faced the

WHEN I LOOKED BACK FROM HENRY FOWLER TO THE GROUP, I CAUGHT THE hint of a signal from Dr. Nickleson, a subtle hand gesture.

Fowler continued to cry. Loud long cries that bordered on screams. The kids looked terrified. Hell, we were all terrified. He kept peeking up at us—checking. Meanwhile, I was looking everywhere—searching for anything that might help get this poor family out of here before he opened fire.

Nickleson and his wife were now standing next to each other. I took a step toward them.

In a whisper, Diana said, "Is there anything you can do? Anything we can do? Anything?"

My instincts told me that Nickleson was a decent person. Now he proved it. He disobeyed Fowler's strict no-talking rule. "Don't worry about me or Diana. Just help the kids. They don't deserve this."

I said quietly, "Nobody deserves this. I'll do everything I can."

For now, I had no chance of disarming Fowler. If I even tried, we'd end up with corpses everywhere, and

I'd be on the bottom of the pile. I was thinking that I had to get out of this house again. I'd talked to Fowler face-to-face, and I'd seen the hostages. For the moment, they were all right. *I had to get the hell out of the house.* If I did, now that I knew the layout, the state of the hostages, we might be able to find a way to get back in, or to pick off Fowler—

His crying stopped suddenly.

"What the fuck are you assholes talking about?" he shouted.

The Glock was in his hand, raised toward us. His palm loosely clutched the grip. His index finger was poised against the trigger.

"I said, *No talking.* And I meant *No talking.* And I meant it especially for you," Fowler said as he pointed his gun at Dr. Nickleson.

I knew enough to be quiet now. Anything I'd say might set Fowler off.

"Okay, recreation time is officially over. Everyone get back down on the floor," Fowler said. "On the floor. On the floor." He kept saying it like a chant, like a cheer. "On the floor. On the floor."

As exhausted as they were, they all scrambled to get down. I don't think that Dr. Nickleson moved more slowly than the others. But what I thought made no difference. Nickleson wasn't moving fast enough for Henry Fowler.

"You know, quack, I've decided that you just don't know how to take orders. And that's just not very help-ful in a tense hostage situation like this."

HENRY FOWLER EXTENDED HIS ARM AND AIMED THE GUN DIRECTLY AT DR. Nickleson.

"Henry, don't be crazy!" Diana shouted.

"Daddy!" Chloe yelled. "Don't shoot Barry. Please, Daddy."

"I hear you, sweetheart," he said.

Then Fowler pulled the trigger and shot Nickleson.

The doctor fell to his knees. His bright-green sweater became a sponge for the blood seeping out of him. Then Nickleson slumped to his side.

Instinctively Diana rose and pushed her husband onto his back. I rushed a sofa pillow under his legs.

"Get the hell away from him!" Fowler yelled. "Don't you dare help him. You never helped me when I was hurting."

Diana screamed, "You filthy animal!" at Fowler. And she ignored him.

Jeremy, Chloe, and Trey were crying. Melissa was on her knees. She was trying desperately to catch her breath.

I knew that there was no such thing as a "good" bullet wound, but a stomach wound was really bad. It could kill in a few minutes. A bullet could explode the colon, abdomen, liver, arteries. Fecal matter could splatter into the system and cause an infection that wouldn't stop. Bones could shatter into the kidneys, into the spleen.

"I said to get the hell away from him!" Fowler shouted again. "I mean it!"

I thought it was a matter of seconds until he put a bullet into Diana or me, or both of us.

It was also clear to me that Diana didn't care what her former husband did. Her instincts of love and decency had taken over. She obviously loved Barry Nickleson very much.

"If you think I'm going to let Barry bleed out, you're crazier than I thought," she said. "What do we do to help Barry?" she asked me.

"Pull the sweater and shirt up. Gently. Don't try to take any clothes off of him. Pull gently. Gently."

Nickleson's eyes suddenly opened. I was hoping it was a good sign. It wasn't. The eyes rolled aimlessly, then fell shut again.

Diana didn't have to pull up much of the shirt and sweater before I saw the entry wound. It was to the far right of the navel, closer to his side. That was good news. The bad news was that blood was flowing out quickly, puddling onto the carpet, seeping down his pants. I helped Diana press hard on the wound. The hairs on Nickleson's stomach, the ones that weren't covered with blood, had literally been singed by the bullet.

"Get up, Diana!" Fowler screamed. "I said, *Get up.*" She didn't move, just kept applying pressure to the wound.

Fowler moved his gun from Diana's head...to the middle of my forehead.

"Get up, Cross. Or you're dead for Christmas."

Diana nodded frantically. I stood. As I did I glanced down at Nickleson's bloody belly. It looked like the bleeding had slowed, or maybe I was just hoping for some kind of miracle.

"Get out of this house," Fowler said to me. "Get out of this house right now, or I'll kill you."

I took a step back and felt my shoes sink into the bloody carpet. I turned and started toward the hallway. Fowler walked behind me. I unlocked the door and opened it.

I had taken in everything I could inside the house. Now I needed a plan to rescue the six hostages. I had to talk to the others on our team.

The snow was still coming down. Would it ever end? Would this nightmare ever end?

"I want you to notice this, Cross. Unlike the doctor, you didn't do anything bad to me. So I won't do anything to you. See? I'm basically a decent guy."

CHAPTER
17

WHEN I HAD GONE INTO THE HOUSE AT FOUR A.M., THE SNOW WAS UP TO MY ankles. Coming out at seven, I realized it was up to my knees.

I couldn't count the number of cops and others standing outside now, but this was clearly the media event of the day. Hey, what was Christmas without a hostage crisis?

On the far side of the street, to the right of the police van, was just about every local reporter I'd ever seen. Also network trucks and electronic generators, technicians, makeup people, lighting experts.

To the left of the van were folks from the neighborhood. There were even some kids. *Shouldn't they be home opening gifts?* Several folks had camera phones held high above their heads. They clicked away. They texted. They tweeted.

But it was the MPD people who blew me away. There must have been fifty rank-and-file men and women at the scene. They held pistols and four-foot-high shields. The snipers were still at their posts in the neighboring houses, but now three SWAT members had positioned themselves at the port of danger—the front of the house. They were squatted flat against the limestone.

I had another small problem: how was I going to get through the snow blocking me in?

I heard a voice from the crowd. "Hey, Merry Christmas, Detective!"

I didn't acknowledge the shout-out, but I noticed a smattering of applause, a few whistles.

Then I heard a woman's voice—coming from close *behind me.*

"Mr. Cross," she said. "Detective."

I spun around to look at the front door. It was partially open. Standing there was Melissa Brandywine—sad, stunned, still shaking like a leaf. She was leaning against the door frame with her left hand. Her right was hidden behind the door itself.

"Mr. Cross…this is for you. Henry told me…to give it to you."

She brought her right arm out from behind the door. And handed me a snow shovel.

Book Two

SCARY CHRISTMAS

CHAPTER
18

"WELL, LOOK WHO GOT OUT IN ONE PIECE," ADAM NU SAID. THEN HE GAVE me a quick hug that wasn't like him at all.

I let out a breath. "Yeah, it wasn't a lot of fun. I'll start on the details of what's going on inside, and then maybe we can get a plan going. But if I don't get some hot coffee I'm going to be useless," I said.

Nu sent McGoey to get me something to eat, a smart use of the detective's time.

"Alex, let me tell you about the follow-up ID we got about fifteen minutes ago," Nu said. He pressed a few buttons on his laptop.

The Styrofoam cup McGoey handed me felt so nice and warm in my hands that I almost didn't want to drink it. Almost. He'd also brought a sandwich—Christmas dinner.

"You remember that girl from the first report, the one they couldn't ID?" Nu said.

"Yeah." I nodded. "All they had was 'Patty' as the name."

"Well, they've got a name and background check now," Nu said. I waited for the fill-ins.

"Name is Patricia Kocot. Originally from Maine. Came to DC after high school. Got a secretary job at Treasury. Pretty, popular. Until she started using Ecstasy. Then coke, then horse…"

"Then Henry Fowler," I said.

"You got it. They found her an hour ago in her room. She had four bullets in her head."

I swallowed the last of a ham and egg on white. I'd had no idea how hungry I was.

Then McGoey jumped in. "Tell Cross what the ME said."

"Oh yeah. When I spoke to the ME on the phone, he told me Patricia Kocot was killed around noon yesterday. Then he said, 'Whoever did it must have been very angry, or crazy, or both.' "

I shoved my crumbled sandwich wrapper into the Styrofoam coffee cup. I shot the cup at the paper garbage bag a few feet away. Missed by a mile. The day was going like that.

"Both!" I said to Nu. "He's angry and crazy."

As I walked over to retrieve the cup, I heard what should have been one of the most beautiful sounds in the world, church bells—loud and rich and joyful. Christmas morning was here, wasn't it? And so was I. Miles and miles from home.

I turned back to Nu and McGoey. "Let's go over everything I saw in there. Let's get a plan to put Fowler down."

CHAPTER
19

on Christmas.

The first thing she did was dial up the thermostat and "put up the coffee," as she liked to say. Then she brought a big CVS shopping bag into the living room and got started on the stockings. Filling the stockings was her job. And everybody seemed to enjoy the inexpensive gifts as much as the pricier shirts and sweaters and books and electronic games.

Nana doled out the tiny plastic puzzles and Hershey bars and ballpoint pens. In her tried-and-true manner, the stocking gifts had a double meaning. She gave Bree a disposable lighter. It was Nana's way of telling her that she knew Bree sneaked an occasional cigarette.

Nana put a bottle of OPI nail polish in Ava's stocking, thinking it might inspire the girl to stop biting her nails.

She dropped iPod earbuds into Damon's stocking. A bright-red hair clip went into Jannie's. Markers for Ali. And the "one-handed flosser" was for Alex.

"Alex," she said softly. Then she looked out the front window. The snow had finally stopped. But there was still no sign of Alex.

"My, my," she heard someone say. "Santa's helpers get younger and prettier every year."

Nana turned around and saw Bree standing at the edge of the living room. They hugged and wished each other a Merry Christmas, both of them knowing it wasn't all that merry without Alex in the house.

"Did you get any sleep?" Nana asked.

"Not a wink."

"Makes two of us," Nana said. "Terrible knot in my stomach all night."

A few minutes later Jannie and Damon and Ali and Ava joined them. Everyone smiled and hugged and wished one another a Merry Christmas, but the usual rush to rip open gifts just wasn't there.

"What this Christmas morning needs is a good hot breakfast," Nana finally said.

They all pretended to agree with her.

"Well, let's get into the kitchen and get to work. You don't think I'm going to fix a big breakfast all by myself," said Nana. "I need helpers."

The children followed her into the kitchen. Bree said she'd join them in a minute. "I love cracking eggs. Save that job for me," she called after them.

Then she picked up the remote and flicked on the television. Words at the bottom of the screen said CHRISTMAS HOSTAGE CRISIS.

There was a shot of the big, handsome house in

Georgetown. Snow and people and cops were every-where. The camera then went to three men standing near a police van. Bree immediately recognized Adam Nu. She didn't recognize a red-haired man in a green ski jacket. But she sure knew the somber-looking one standing next to him, rubbing his hands together against the cold.

She spoke softly, as if the TV could hear her. "Oh, Alex, Alex, Alex."

Then she immediately changed the channel.

But Channel 4 had the identical scene. That net-work, however, featured a newscaster with a micro-phone in the foreground. She was talking to the camera.

"From lawyer to drug addict to madman—that's the road Henry Fowler took to arrive here this Christmas morning…"

Bree quickly turned off the television. She rubbed her sleeve against her damp eyes.

Then she shouted, "I'm coming in now. Nobody better have touched those eggs!"

CHAPTER
20

"PANCAKES OR WAFFLES?" NANA ASKED IN A VOICE SO CHEERFUL THAT everybody knew it was a put-on. Add to it the fact that both Jannie (always pro-waffle) and Damon (fiercely pro-pancake) said they didn't really care. It was obvious that worry about Alex had pretty much sucked the joy right out of the holiday.

"It's Christmas," Nana finally said. "Why don't I just make both? Pancakes *and* waffles coming up!"

No response came from the kids.

Suddenly Nana yanked off her apron and flung it to the kitchen floor. "Damn!" she shouted. Nana saying the word *damn* got everyone's attention.

"Now, you all listen to me. I don't like this terrible situation any more than you do. I've got a grandson who's missing for Christmas. Does it make me gloomy? Does it make me angry? Does it make me sad? The answer to all three of those questions is yes. It certainly does. My heart's as heavy as yours. I could burst into tears any minute. Fact is, I did, twice last night, and I may do it again. But the truth is…life has to be lived.

This Christmas is today. Now. *This* Christmas will never come again. And I don't mean to be preaching a holiday sermon, but Christmas is about hope and faith. And we'd all better realize that, you hear me?"

There was silence in the room. Only the sound of bacon in the frying pan.

"I said, *You hear me?*"

"It's hard to do, Nana," said Jannie, "when you feel sick to your stomach. The worst thing is, lots of folks make fun of policemen."

"I don't disagree with any of that," Nana said. "If it were easy I wouldn't have to be delivering this lecture."

"Okay, Nana," Bree said, and she squeezed her shoulders and gave her a kiss.

"Now," Nana said, "whoever dropped my apron on the floor, please pick it up and give it to me." Everyone laughed…a little.

"Then we'll have a real fine breakfast. And then we'll go into the living room, and we'll each open up one gift. And then…"

"Then what?" Ava asked.

"Then Damon will go out and shovel the front walk. *So we can all get to church.*"

While Damon was moaning and the others were laughing, Nana walked back into the living room for a moment. She stared out the front window. Still no sign of Alex. This was the worst Christmas in her long, long memory. She couldn't bear to lose that man.

CHAPTER
21

McGOEY AND NU SPOKE IN ALMOST PERFECT UNISON.

"You answer it, Alex."

A call was coming from inside the hostage house. I picked up the phone, and our conversation came through the speakers.

"Alex Cross," I said.

"I'm disappointed in you, Cross" came Henry Fowler's voice. "I'm very, very disappointed."

"And the reason is?"

"You betrayed me. I just looked out the living room window, and to the left of your van I saw two police officers...armoring up."

I said nothing.

"You still there, Cross?"

"I'm still here. I'm still listening."

"Now. Were they putting on those protective vests because they were chilly, or"—and now he started screaming—*"because they're going to come shooting their way into my house? Because I'm telling—"*

"Cool it, Fowler." I raised my voice, but only slightly.

"You're in there with an arsenal of handguns and rifles. You didn't think we'd armor up for protection?"

A pause, and then, "That's a fairly intelligent lie, Cross. But I do want to add—and I hope you're listening well—at the first sign of a home invasion, there'll be six dead hostages near the twinkly Christmas tree."

"We've got nothing that stupid planned." I watched McGoey roll his eyes.

"Perfect," Fowler said. He seemed calm enough now that I could pose the question I most wanted to ask.

"By the way, how's the doctor doing?"

"On the mend," he said. "He'll be up and about in no time." Then he directed himself to Nickleson. "That's the expression, Doc, isn't it? Up and about in no time? Hey, how about another *shot* of rotgut? Get it—*rotgut?*"

A pause, and then, "See you around, Cross."

Click.

I looked at Nu and McGoey. Then I spoke.

"We'd better get moving before he does. Fowler is crazier than ever."

And that was really saying something.

CHAPTER
22

THE THREE OF US MOVED TO THE LEFT OF THE VAN AND LOOKED AT THE house. I guess we felt that if we stared at the place hard enough, we might be inspired to come up with a brilliant plan—that wouldn't end with dead hostages.

No inspiration took place. But something else happened.

It was McGoey who noticed it. He elbowed me in the side and said, "The front door is opening."

Nu and I looked. Sure enough, I could see that the door was cracked open. Then it closed. Then it opened again.

Now it was opening even more. Suddenly it was flung wide by someone, and Melissa Brandywine—completely disheveled, her eyes filled with fear—came quickly stumbling out, tripping, falling, rising up again, running toward the police van. She looked behind her, and the door remained open.

In her bare feet she ran as best she could on the path that I'd cleared earlier. I hoped to God she wasn't about to get shot in the back.

I rushed to the end of the path, motioning everyone else to stand back. This might be some sort of insane trick by Fowler.

Melissa Brandywine started to sob hysterically. I scooped her up and carried her behind the van. Someone from EMT aimed a space heater at her. They covered her with blankets. They massaged an antibiotic into her feet.

"Detective," she said, but no more words came out. She began to sob.

"Four mgs of Valium'll calm her down," one of the EMTs said.

"Go for it."

Within seconds he had a syringe in her arm.

Melissa's breathing got more rhythmic, calmer. She looked up at me.

"Henry told me to tell you…when he let me out…he said…well, exactly…here's the quote: 'Tell Cross this is a goodwill gesture. Wish him Happy Holidays.' "

"At least one person is safe," I said. Melissa nodded. The Valium could only do so much for her, but it was clearly helping.

"How's Dr. Nickleson?" I asked.

She shook her head. "Not good. He's not bleeding too much. But he's still on the floor, and he isn't moving. I don't know. I can't tell. I think he's breathing."

I flipped open my cell phone and tapped in the hostage-house number.

"Cross," Fowler said. "No need for a thank-you

phone call. When you have the time, a simple e-mail will do."

"I want to come in again—with medical personnel. Let us take Dr. Nickleson out of there. He desperately needs help," I said. "Don't let him die."

"Did Missy tell you that the doc needs help? Here's some advice for you. Never believe what a whore says."

"I want to take Dr. Nickleson out of there," I said.

Fowler began to scream. The screaming was so loud that I could hear his words coming from the house—even as they came through the phone.

"I don't care what you want! I want what I want! Nickleson's going to die! Got that? He's going to die! He's going to die for what he did to me! He took my life from me! Now I'm going to take his! I'm going to kill all of them."

CHAPTER
23

I TURNED TO McGOEY AND NU. "I'VE GOT TO GO BACK IN THERE. WE HAVE TO get the doctor out now. Maybe I have a plan."

"And that plan is?" McGoey asked suspiciously. "What are you holding back?"

I told Nu and McGoey what I had in mind, but that was only *if* Fowler let me in the house again. I didn't know if that would happen.

I hustled over to grab a body-armor vest from SWAT. I told them my plan as they hooked and harnessed me in.

Then I phoned Fowler and told him I was coming in. I didn't ask permission this time. He was almost trancelike in his speech. Down in the valley of despair again. That was troubling. Maybe the combination of drugs and fatigue had finally got to him. I didn't know, and it really didn't matter.

"That's not such a good idea, Cross," he finally said, "coming back in here."

"Why's that?"

"I may not let you out this time." Then Fowler hung up on me.

I looked over at Adam Nu. "He said, *Come on down!*"

"*The Price Is Right,*" Nu said with a crooked grin. "I sure hope the price isn't your life, Alex."

For the second time, I crossed the street to the sidewalk in front of the house on 30th Street NW. The newscasters and onlookers had been cleared as far back as two hundred feet. That was beyond the possible effective radius of a small hand-grenade explosion in a residential area. Only the van and the MPD officers, the medics and the snipers, were allowed to remain any closer to the house. I felt lonely as I walked the icy pathway. And kind of sad. But this was my job.

What did I have going for me? A bulletproof vest and a plan that might work, or might blow up in my face. A few hours ago when I walked here, the sky was black and the snow was falling fast. Now it was light out. A pale winter sun lit the entire street. Everything felt more substantial and real.

I felt a sudden quiver in my arms. With every step I could sense my resolve growing weaker.

The front door opened a few inches. Strangely, the sounds I'd come to associate with the house were all gone. There was no weeping, no screaming, no sound of children's voices. Even the crazy man who ran the show was silent.

My sense of time was skewed. The few seconds it took to walk the pathway felt a lot longer than that. It seemed like the steps to the door took at least a minute. I knew that wasn't accurate.

Then I was looking up at Henry Fowler, who was holding a rifle on me. "Cross, I think you're making a big mistake," he said.

"Maybe you're right."

"No *maybe*. I...am...right. Now you're a dead man too. Come on in."

CHAPTER
24

BECAUSE IT WAS CHRISTMAS MORNING, A SPECIAL DAY, NANA AGREED TO make her "sweet bacon." The recipe: thick bacon first fried in a cast-iron skillet, then covered with brown sugar and baked in the oven.

"I only cook sweet bacon for a holiday or a birthday," she always said. That was the rule of the house. *Her* house, she insisted, even though Alex had bought and paid for it.

Once, when Damon pointed out that Arbor Day was a real holiday, Nana agreed with him. And she changed the rule. Now it read: "I only cook sweet bacon for a *major* holiday or a birthday."

Waffles. Pancakes. Cheese grits. And sweet bacon.

"There may be no need to cook the turkey later on," Bree said. "This meal could last me the whole day. Maybe the whole week."

"You speak for yourself," Damon said. "I'll be ready for turkey and mashed potatoes in an hour or so. And those yams I love with the mini-marshmallows."

The maple syrup was soaking into the waffles and

pancakes. The sweet-bacon strips were crunchy crisp. And the mood was finally cheerful.

Then Jannie spoke. "You know, it seems to me there's only one thing missing from this breakfast table."

They all immediately thought of Alex. A somber mood reinvaded the room. There was quiet. Nana squeezed her lips together to keep from tearing up. Bree looked out the window of the kitchen door.

Damon shot a "Why'd you make everyone feel bad again?" look at Jannie. She realized that her comment—made innocently—had upset everyone. She said, "Oh no! Listen. Listen. What I meant was…what's missing are those ridiculous reindeer antlers and the flickering electric red nose that Damon puts on every Christmas."

"Oh, I forgot all about those stupid…those *stunning* antlers," Nana said.

"Get outta here," Damon said. "That's not happening. *You* wear the antlers. Nana can wear the antlers."

"Nobody wears those antlers like you," Jannie said, and Ali giggled.

"Oh please, can I see them on you? Oh *please*," said Ava.

"I don't even know where those dumb things are," Damon said.

"Lucky for us, I do," said Jannie. "I've got them right here."

And out from under her chair she produced a pair of cloth antlers that were sewn into a headband and decorated with a sprig of plastic holly. She also had a tiny red lightbulb attached to a big rubber band that would fit snugly around Damon's head.

Then Nana said, "Before we see Damon dressed like a reindeer, let's join hands and say a prayer."

They held hands and bowed their heads. Nana spoke.

"Dear Lord, Who on this blessed Christmas Day brought Your Son into the world, we ask You to look with kindness on another son. Your son Alex. As he strives to help others we ask You to help him. To keep him from harm. To protect him from evil. According to Your holy will."

Then together the Cross family said, "Amen."

FOWLER KEPT HIS HAND FIRMLY ON HIS RIFLE. HE ALSO KEPT HIS EYES ON me as I surveyed the wreckage of the room. The good, the bad, the very ugly.

All three children were lying on the floor. They seemed to be sleeping. I sure hoped they were.

The next thing I noticed made my stomach drop—*the sandwiches were gone.*

Fowler knew exactly what I was thinking. I sometimes forgot how smart he was, how observant of everything around him.

"If you're looking for the sandwiches, Cross, don't get your panties in a twist. Diana was so freaking scared that I'd shove the peanut butter down their throats, she ate them herself. The kids aren't dead yet. They could be, but they're not. I guess they just got tired of waiting up for Santa." He laughed.

The room was a battle site, even worse than just a few hours before. A red velvet club chair had been viciously slashed open. A mahogany end table had been broken up and the pieces burned in the fireplace.

"*Hate* red velvet," Fowler said about the club chair. "She bought it anyway. Never listens to me."

Diana sat cross-legged on the floor with her husband's head resting on her lap. She looked pale and exhausted. But the doctor looked a whole lot worse. He lay motionless, his eyes closed. This was a life-or-death situation, and I had a good idea which side of the equation Nickleson was on right now.

I moved over and took Nickleson's neck pulse. It was slow, erratic, but it was *there.*

"Listen, Fowler, we've got to get him some help."

"Listen, Cross…no." Then he went into another one of his rages.

"You're like everybody else here, Cross. *Nobody listens.* Or if they do happen to listen, they don't understand what I'm saying. And what I'm saying is that *he's going to die anyway.* I could plug another bullet into his belly to finish the job, but I want him to suffer and then fade away, slowly bleed, slowly wind down like a goddamn toy. Yeah, a toy. Like that stupid electric poodle that Chloe has. Bark-bark-bark. Then two barks, then one bark, then no bark."

I found myself shaking my head in amazement at the level of his venom and anger. Diana, on the other hand, was weary and close to collapse. She ignored Fowler and just kept gently stroking Nickleson's pale hand.

"Fowler, look," I said. "I told you I wanted to hear your story. I still do. I have the general picture. Now I want the details. But first I've got to help this very sick man." Maybe Henry Fowler believed me. Who the hell knew with him? I had no idea from one minute to the next what he was thinking.

Suddenly I grabbed a bottle of Absolut Vodka from the scattered broken piles of gifts near the tree. The vodka bottle was unbroken and unopened. A green silk ribbon was wrapped around the neck.

I also pulled a white Paul Stuart dress shirt from its gift box. I tossed the shirt to Diana and said, "Get the straight pins out of this thing. I need to use the shirt to cleanse his wound."

"What the hell are you doing, Cross? Just what the hell are you doing?"

I turned back to Fowler. "However this all turns out, it'll be better without a murder charge on your hands. I want to help Nickleson make it through."

Henry Fowler narrowed his eyes slightly. He seemed to be thinking about what I said, or maybe he was just getting punchy from whatever he was on.

Chloe and Jeremy were awake now. They watched their mother, father, and me as if they were watching a scary horror movie.

"All the pins are out of the shirt," Diana said. "What now?"

"Just hold on to the shirt for a second," I said. "We're going to help your husband."

CHAPTER
26

I KNELT BESIDE DR. NICKLESON. THEN I TWISTED OPEN THE CAP ON THE Absolut. I poured about a cup of the stuff over the bullet-shot area. The sting of the vodka hit the wound and apparently startled the doctor awake for a few seconds. Nickleson's eyes opened, but they didn't focus. Then they closed again. Diana leaned in closer to him and whispered, "I love you, Barry."

She didn't whisper softly enough. Fowler heard it too, and her words destroyed any sense of calm her former husband might have been feeling.

Fowler lifted his rifle and fired…right through the ceiling, almost directly over his head. It was deafening, and it made a large hole.

"Get away from him right now, Cross, or you're going to have a hole in you."

The phone rang, and I grabbed it. "*No one is hurt!* This is Cross," I said. Then I hung right up.

"Who told you to answer the phone?" Fowler barked.

"Give me a minute with the doctor, just a minute," I said. "Please."

Maybe it was the word *please* that brought Fowler back to a few seconds of sanity. "Do what you want," he said. "Take the bullet out with a steak knife and fork."

I took the shirt from Diana. Then I ripped it in half.

The vodka acted not only as an antibacterial but also as a solvent to wash away some of the caked blood. I dabbed as gently as I could. Already some blood was oozing from the wound. I didn't want to make the situation worse.

"Okay, Cross. Your minute is up."

"Almost finished," I said.

Then Fowler began one of his repetitive rants: "Time's up! Time's up! Time's up! Time's up!"

The light in the room was scarce—no lamps. His screaming was borderline insane. The twins were cowering against the fireplace. I couldn't tell if the wound was infected. But my diagnosis made no difference. This was about as primitive as a Civil War battlefield.

"Time's up, Cross! The goddamn time is goddamn up!"

Again Fowler shot his rifle, this time through the wall near the living room entrance. I tried to ignore the chaos around me—the crying kids, the moaning victim, the screaming madman, the rifle, the disorder, the fact that it was Christmas. And church bells were ringing again.

So was the phone! This time Fowler took it. "We're fine!" Then he hung up.

I took the clean half of the shirt and twisted it loosely into a sort of rope. I lifted Nickleson gently and slipped the shirt-rope under him, then tied it securely around him. The shirt-rope was barely long enough, but it tied. Nickleson was a skinny man. That was the only piece of good luck I'd had in the last twenty-four hours.

"You think your Boy Scout first aid is going to help him?" Fowler shouted at me. "This asshole is dead or dying. And you just wasted perfectly good vodka on him."

I stood up. I'd done all I could for Nickleson.

Then I watched as Fowler thrust a hand into his right pants pocket. A moment later he was holding a palmful of pills. He shoved them into his mouth. Then he chewed and swallowed them like a starving man.

"Visiting the OxyContinent, Fowler?"

"Just a short trip," he said. "Hey. I'm already back again. See me? See the grin? I'm right here."

I knew that on his drug menu OxyContin was probably just a midmorning snack.

Then he looked straight at me. The rifle was by his side. Dust from the ceiling plaster fell down on him as…as gently as snow.

"And by the way, Cross, I did want to add one thing about me and my occasional usage of the big *O*…"

"What's that?"

He walked out from under the plaster flakes and came toward me. He lifted the rifle so that it touched my chin. With his face so close that our noses were almost touching, he screamed as loudly as a man could scream.

"*Mind…your…own…fucking…business!*"

CHAPTER
27

THEN FOWLER STOPPED TALKING. TO ME, AND TO HIS FAMILY.

Henry Fowler's icy silence was even scarier than Henry Fowler's crazy ranting.

He sat on the edge of the big red chair with the ripped seat pillow. His only movement was turning his head from Diana to the doctor to the children. Finally he'd end up staring the longest at me. A few hours passed. I had to say something.

The OxyContin had calmed him down a little, but I knew that it would eventually lead to uncontrolled elation, and in Fowler's case that could lead to uncontrolled shooting.

"So what's next, Fowler?" I asked.

Softly, almost sounding drunk, he said, "You tell me. You tell me."

"I've got no plans," I said.

"Then maybe we'll just spend the rest of our lives together in here. That'd be sweet, huh? Spend whatever time we have left together. Maybe hold hands?"

I said nothing, and he went back to watching us.

A few more minutes passed. Fowler seemed to be growing foggier, and weaker. If I was ever going to take him down, the time was getting close. I thought I could handle Fowler. It was his partner that worried me—the AR-15 carbine rifle. Fowler stroked and petted it as if it were the faithful family dog.

Time to get moving.

Somehow, I needed Fowler out of the living room and in the hallway that led to the kitchen. I waited a few more minutes. He stared at me, and I stared back. Finally I spoke. "You want to talk, Fowler? I think we should."

"You mean, like, have a conversation? Man-to-man?"

"Yeah. Serious. Private."

He smiled at me. That nasty, crooked smirk of his.

"Sure. What do you want to talk about? Football? Politics? Women?"

"I want to talk about *you*," I said.

Suddenly he stood up and yelled, "That's my favorite fucking subject!"

"I want to hear the truth," I said. "I want to know what your former wife and Nickleson did to hurt you so badly. The details. Your side of the story."

This was the crucial moment. If he believed I was interested in what he had to say, I had a chance. If he thought I was lying, I'd be shot—and down on the floor next to the doctor.

He looked up and stared at the bullet hole in the ceiling. He was deciding.

"Let's go talk. In the kitchen or even just down the hallway," I said.

Suddenly Fowler was screaming again. "How stupid do you think I am? Yeah, we'll go talk, and then these bastards'll take off." He gestured to Diana and Nickleson and the children.

Diana immediately spoke up.

"Don't be crazy, Henry," she said. "If I left, then Barry would be as good as gone. I would never leave Barry here alone with you. You'd kill him for sure."

"You're damn right I would. Or maybe just shoot him in the gut again."

When Fowler spoke his voice was almost cheerful. The sudden alertness in his eyes gave me hope that he was going to do this my way.

"Let's go for a walk, Cross," he said. "We can talk in the den. Man-to-man."

The den wasn't a good choice for me. The hallway was where I wanted us to be.

"How about the kitchen?" I asked. "I could use something cold to drink."

He shrugged his shoulders.

"Sure. We aim to please," he said. That line was so funny, he cracked himself up.

We walked to the living room entranceway. Fowler stopped there and then spun around. He held his rifle in the air. For a moment I thought he might fire at the ceiling again.

Instead he spoke to his family with quiet contempt. "I swear to God, if anyone in here moves, I'm going to paint the walls with your blood."

CHAPTER
28

FOWLER AND I SLOWLY WALKED DOWN THE LONG HALLWAY THAT CONNECTED
the front of the house with the kitchen. We went past
the dining room.

I wanted to get him down that hallway and as close
to the kitchen as possible. But anything could go wrong.
What if Diana defied Fowler and tried to get out? What
if she tried to run with her kids? The phrase "paint the
walls with your blood" kept echoing in my head.

What if Fowler decided to kill me now? Out of sight
of his children. Away from the front of the house. What
if he was planning to escape—and use me as a hostage?

The hallway was narrow and mostly unlit. In the darkness it looked like the walls were covered with drawings,
school sports citations, vacation photographs.

"Is there a light switch here someplace?" I asked.

"I know where I'm going."

"I don't," I said.

"You don't need to."

We were about ten feet away from the kitchen when
Fowler stopped short. He grabbed my shoulder. Something had set him off again. My body went rigid.

"Here! Go ahead, Cross! *Here!*" he said. "Take a look right here!" He twisted me to my right and pushed me hard, almost headfirst against the wall.

"C'mon, look. *Look at the most beautiful picture in the world!*"

I was so close to the wall that all I could see was a blur of dark paneling and a light-wood picture frame.

Fowler kept yelling at me to look. So I forced my head back a few inches to bring the picture into focus. My eyes began to adjust to the dark.

"Just look at this photo. I took it, man. I'm the photographer."

The moment I saw the photograph, I understood some of Fowler's madness. One picture was worth a thousand rants.

The photo: Fowler's family sitting on the deck of a house. It was probably somewhere on the New England shore. Maybe Jersey. A few years ago, I imagined.

He continued to yell. "See how perfect they all look, how…how…blond they are. It's like a clothes catalog…Brooks Brothers…Ralph Lauren….You know where that is? That's Martha's Vineyard…Oak Bluffs….See that house? I rented that house. That house cost me eighty thousand dollars for the month of August. Eighty thousand dollars. Twenty a week. Most people don't make eighty grand in a year. And that's what I was spending on a damn rental in Martha's Vineyard. Those were the days, man. Those were the days, my friend. We thought they'd never end."

CHAPTER
29

I FOCUSED ON THE PHOTOGRAPH THAT HENRY FOWLER HAD TAKEN. ALL three children were wearing charcoal-blue Shetland sweaters. The youngest appeared to be no more than two, smiling in his mother's arms. And Fowler was right. They looked good. They were blond. They were deeply tanned. Diana's hair was shorter, and everyone else's hair was longer. Diana looked beautiful.

They sat smiling very naturally in front of a great big weather-beaten ocean-side house. Everyone looked truly happy, facing the man who was taking the picture. Henry Fowler. Daddy dearest.

"God, what a summer. How we loved it there, all of us! We had a pool with an ocean view. We had a sail-boat. Two college kids crewed for us. Every day we ate lobster and fries and clams and blueberry pie. À la mode. I burned money. *Burned* money! Thought it would never end."

Fowler's screaming had risen into a kind of tearful shout. His words were loud, but now they were filled with nose and throat noises, and his tears. I didn't like him any better, but I was beginning to understand him.

"I didn't mind burning the money. And you know why I didn't mind, Cross? Because I loved my life. I loved it so much. I was so lucky. I loved my life. Yeah, I knew what I was then. I was the luckiest guy in the whole goddamn world. I loved my goddamn family."

He brought the level of his voice down a little. It was filled with bitterness and anger. All he said was "And then…and then…we blew it."

He stopped talking and lifted his rifle up toward the ceiling.

He held the gun high like that for a few seconds. Then he slowly brought it down to his side.

As Fowler let the rifle drop, I saw what I had been waiting for. My chance.

A small red light was shining right in the middle of Fowler's chest.

The plan I'd made with the sharpshooters was taking shape. In seconds a bullet would follow that light, and this long Christmas nightmare would be over.

"Let's go," Fowler said quietly. "Let's have our talk, Cross."

The red light stayed at the center of Fowler's chest. He was as good as dead.

Then I did something that had never been part of the plan. I just couldn't stop myself. This was in my DNA.

With all my strength I grabbed Fowler's shoulders

and spun him to the floor. I knew I was going to get shot. No way out of it. But the gun didn't go off.

Fowler fell, and I collapsed on top of him. Man-to-man.

His head whacked the floor, and blood came spurting from his nose. He shouted, "You sonofabitch!" Then I heard a crash, the shatter of glass.

The sniper's bullet pierced the kitchen window and spun through the airspace above us.

The bullet missed Henry Fowler.

He was alive.

I had saved this madman's life.

CHAPTER
30

I DROVE MY KNEE HARD INTO FOWLER'S BACK. I PULLED BOTH ARMS UP and around him until I felt that they were ready to snap. Fowler wasn't going anyplace. He also wasn't talking. Just crying, blubbering like a little kid.

Within seconds everyone who was outside the house was suddenly inside. Adam Nu and three of his men ran to me. They snapped cuffs and leg restraints on Fowler. They pulled him up off the floor and shoved him down the hallway.

"*Hold it!*" Fowler shouted. Just like he'd been screaming commands all day.

"Keep moving," Nu said. "Shut the hell up."

"No. Wait a second, Adam," I said. "What is it, Fowler? What do you want?"

"Why didn't you let your sniper shoot me? Why?" he asked.

"It was a Christmas gift."

"I don't need any gift from you. Or anybody else."

"Maybe not. But it wasn't meant for you. It was for your children. I didn't want them to see their father's body being carried away on Christmas."

"Merry Christmas, Cross," Fowler whispered then. "For what it's worth."

"Get him out of here," I said.

Then Adam Nu and I walked into the living room. McGoey was getting a handle on the situation. The EMTs were working on Nickleson—syringes and IVs, and a gurney coming through the front door. Two EMT guys slid a board under the badly wounded man. They carefully hoisted him onto the gurney and carried him out.

Social workers were talking to the kids—wiping faces, feeding them fruit, getting them to the bathroom. Diana followed the gurney. She stopped for just a second and turned to me.

"God bless you, Detective."

"Go take care of your husband," I told her.

Police photographers were snapping away at the broken lamps, puddles of blood, every fallen Christmas-tree branch. Outside the house, officers were keeping the news vultures back from the scene. Cameramen and TV reporters with microphones crowded the snowy sidewalk and street. So did the neighborhood looky-loos.

"Somebody close the damn door!" Nu shouted. "It's cold in here."

"Yeah, you've got it rough, Adam," I told him.

Nu smiled and said, "The plan worked. You're a smart guy, Alex."

"What if it hadn't worked?" I asked. "What would you be saying then?"

"I'd be saying, *You're the dumb-ass who got himself shot.*"

McGoey approached us. "The EMTs think Nickleson's got a chance. Bullet missed most of his vitals, and some Boy Scout knew enough to disinfect the wound."

"Yeah," I said. "It's always good to have a Boy Scout around."

The three of us took a last look at the living room. I doubted there was much in that room that hadn't been cracked, smashed, broken, or torn.

"God," said McGoey. "Looks like there was one helluva party here."

"Oh, there was," I said. "It was one helluva party." I shook my head. I felt like I should smile. But I couldn't. I just couldn't.

I looked at my watch. It was almost four in the afternoon. I took out my phone and tapped Bree's name.

"Hey," I said. "Set me a place. And don't let Damon take all the marshmallows off the yams. I'll be home for Christmas."

CHAPTER
31

NEEDLESS TO SAY, IT WAS NANA WHO WOULDN'T GIVE AN INCH. EVERYBODY else rushed over to kiss and hug me when they heard the front door open. Nana remained seated in her chair, her little throne.

"My, my," she finally said. "Is that my grandson over there? Must be a real special occasion that's got him visiting. Oh, I guess it's Christmas."

I walked to her chair and helped her up. We stood with our arms around each other, and I never imagined a woman that size could have so much strength. She nearly squeezed the air right out of me.

"Let's get dinner on the table," she said. "Lord knows it's been sitting in a keep-warm oven long enough."

We headed toward the kitchen. I carried a big bronze-colored turkey to the dining table. Everyone else brought in his or her favorite dish. Damon had the marshmallow yams. Bree had whipped potatoes. Ali brought the cranberry sauce. Ava held the gravy. Jannie carried the stuffing as if she were in a procession.

And, just like every other year, someone had to be asked to bring in the brussels sprouts. That would be me.

We sat at the table with cloth napkins, good china, a little crystal for the Christmas wine.

"Alex," Nana said. That was my signal to say grace. We held hands. Bree squeezed mine so tight that I thought she might never let go.

Then I spoke. "Let us thank the Lord for this meal. And also for our health and happiness. And...for being a good family gathered together like this on Christmas day."

I paused and then said, "Now let us silently give our own personal thanks."

"I'm glad Dad is home!" Ali said in a loud voice, and we all laughed.

"Me too," I said.

We closed our eyes. The room was completely silent. The seconds passed. I had a lot to be thankful for: the safety of our family, my own survival, the joy of—

The prayerful silence was broken by Ava.

"I'm hungry. Doesn't the Lord know it's Christmas?"

We all laughed. And then the bowls and platters of food were passed around. And just as we started to dig in...the phone began to ring.

"Don't you dare pick that up, Alex. *Don't you dare.*"

About the Author

JAMES PATTERSON has had more *New York Times* bestsellers than any other writer, ever, according to *Guinness World Records*. Since his first novel won the Edgar Award in 1977, James Patterson's books have sold more than 240 million copies. He is the author of the Alex Cross novels, the most popular detective series of the past twenty-five years, including *Kiss the Girls* and *Along Came a Spider*. Mr. Patterson also writes the bestselling Women's Murder Club novels, set in San Francisco, and the top-selling New York detective series of all time, featuring Detective Michael Bennett.

James Patterson also writes books for young readers, including the Maximum Ride, Daniel X, Witch & Wizard, and Middle School series. In total, these books have spent more than 220 weeks on national bestseller lists.

His lifelong passion for books and reading led James Patterson to launch the website ReadKiddoRead.com to give adults an easy way to locate the very best books for kids. He writes full-time and lives in Florida with his family.

BOOKS BY JAMES PATTERSON

FEATURING ALEX CROSS

Merry Christmas, Alex Cross • *Kill Alex Cross* • *Cross Fire* • *I, Alex Cross* • *Alex Cross's* Trial (with Richard DiLallo) • *Cross Country* • *Double Cross* • *Cross* • *Mary, Mary* • *London Bridges* • *The Big Bad Wolf* • *Four Blind Mice* • *Violets Are Blue* • *Roses Are Red* • *Pop Goes the Weasel* • *Cat & Mouse* • *Jack & Jill* • *Kiss the Girls* • *Along Came a Spider*

THE WOMEN'S MURDER CLUB

10th Anniversary (with Maxine Paetro) • *The 9th Judgment* (with Maxine Paetro) • *The 8th Confession* (with Maxine Paetro) • *7th Heaven* (with Maxine Paetro) • *The 6th Target* (with Maxine Paetro) • *The 5th Horseman* (with Maxine Paetro) • *4th of July* (with Maxine Paetro) • *3rd Degree* (with Andrew Gross) • *2nd Chance* (with Andrew Gross) • *1st to Die*

FEATURING MICHAEL BENNETT

Tick Tock (with Michael Ledwidge) • *Worst Case* (with Michael Ledwidge) • *Run for Your Life* (with Michael Ledwidge) • *Step on a Crack* (with Michael Ledwidge)

OTHER BOOKS

For previews and information about the author, visit JamesPatterson.com or find him on Facebook or at your app store.